WITCH PIGS

Colin and Jacqui Hawkins

JONATHAN CAPE • LONDON

Deep within the dark bowels of Castle Grimewold the kitchens were seething as preparations were made for Baron de Mugwort's birthday party.

Mrs Slobbersnout, the castle cook, was in a boiling temper.

'Get out of my way,' she hissed at Pea and Pod, the kitchen skivvies. 'And get those pots scrubbed, you useless squealers,' she bellowed.

'Yes, yes, Mrs Slobbersnout,' they squeaked as they began clearing the mountain of greasy pots and pans. The little pigs scrubbed and rubbed until at last, 'We're finished,' whispered Pea as they wearily dried the last pot.

But lurking nearby was sly Ratty Ragworm who had other ideas.

'No, you're not,' he sniggered.

'Watch this!' And he **deliberately** pushed over the great pile of saucepans.

Crash! Crash! Bang!

'You hopeless halfwits,' shouted
Mrs Slobbersnout as she gave the little pigs
a hefty smack around the ears.
'It's not fair,' wailed Pea
and Pod. 'It's not our fault.'

'SHUT UP!'

she roared. 'Get that lot
washed up again!
NOW!'

eanwhile, in the royal chambers, Baron Walter de Mugwort was opening his birthday presents surrounded by his **large** family. The Baron's presents were awful! His wife, Baroness Euphorbia, had knitted him a hideous jumper, and the young Mugworts, Horace and Hortense, had given him very hairy socks and a bottle of *L'Odeur de Sty* after-shave.

'But I didn't want a jumper and I don't shave,' grumbled the Baron.

'I want chocolates, where are my chocs?'

'But you look so sweet in your jumper, Walty dear,' said the Baroness.

'Now I'm just going to see how Cook is getting on with your birthday cake,' and she waddled off, leaving behind a very cross and disgruntled Baron.

Back in the kitchens Pea and Pod's ears were still throbbing. 'How can we get our own back on that sneaky Ratty Ragworm?' asked Pea.

'I know,' said Pod. 'Come on, follow me.' The little pigs hurried along the dust-filled corridors until they arrived at a huge oak door, the entrance to the Sorcery Room of the Grand Witch.

'WHAT'S THE MAGIC WORD?' boomed the door.

'Can you remember the magic word, Pod?' asked Pea.

'Oh . . . fiddlesticks, I can't think,' said Pod.

'FIDDLESTICKS IS INCORRECT,'
shouted the door.
'Oh, poo!' said Pod. 'I didn't
mean that.'
**'POO IS INCORRECT AND A
RUDE WORD,'** roared the door.
'Oh, bum! I didn't mean that,
either,' squeaked Pod.
**'BUM IS INCORRECT AND
AN EVEN RUDER WORD,'**
yelled the door.

'Please think, Pod,' said Pea.
'PLEASE IS THE MAGIC WORD,' rumbled the door. 'Open wide and step
inside,' and it slowly creaked open.
Inside the dark chamber Pea and Pod opened the Great Book of Spells
and searched for one to use on Ratty Ragworm.
'Great, just what we need: the Zany Zit Spell,' giggled Pea as they
concocted a magic potion with some very smelly ingredients.

In the kitchens, Pea and Pod carefully
poured the magic mixture into a
large water jug.
'That'll sort him out,' laughed Pea,
as they put the jug where Ratty Ragworm
was sure to find it.
The kitchens were incredibly hot and
it was not long before Ratty got very thirsty.

He was just about to take a drink, when a sweltering Mrs Slobbersnout cried, 'That's just what I need!' and, to Pea and Pod's horror, she snatched the jug from Ratty and gulped down

every

last

drop.

The spell took effect immediately. Horrible green boils suddenly erupted all over Mrs Slobbersnout, bursting and popping green gunge everywhere.

Pop! Pop! Splot! Erk!

'What's happening?' she squawked.

At that moment the kitchen door crashed open and in strode the Baroness. She was absolutely disgusted to see Cook's boil-bursting performance.

'Get out of the kitchen, you horrid swine,' she shrieked, **'and don't come back until you're fit to be seen!'**

'But . . . but . . . what about the Baron's birthday cake?' said Cook, as an extra large boil on the end of her snout exploded.

'You revolting porker!' screamed the enraged Baroness. 'You cannot make the Baron's cake in that filthy state. **Get out!'**

Mrs Slobbersnout slunk off, with nasty green gunk exploding around her as she went.

The Baroness whirled round, glaring madly. Then her beady gaze fell on Pea and Pod.

'You and you,' she yelled, 'you'll have to make the Baron's cake, and it had better be good, **or you will rot in the deepest, darkest, smelliest dungeons . . . FOR EVER!**'

And with that she swept out of the kitchen, leaving Pea and Pod shivering in fright.

But for once things went well.

'This is easy,' said Pea as he whisked the ingredients together, stirring
everything until it was light and fluffy. They poured the cake mixture into
a tin and then carefully put it into the oven.

Pea turned over the sand-timer. 'When all the sand reaches the bottom of the
glass, the cake will be ready,' he said.

And they sat down by the fire to take a well-earned rest.

However, while Pea and Pod chatted they did not notice Ratty Ragworm
craftily creep up and turn over the sand-timer. 'I think that cake
needs a bit more time,' Ratty sniggered as he
silently slipped back into
the darkness.

Pea and Pod returned to the oven just as the sand in the timer ran through. 'The cake should be ready now!' said Pod as he opened the door. But to their horror thick smoke poured from the oven and billowed around the kitchen.

It was a disaster! The cake was **very** flat, **very** burnt and **very** black.

'Oh no! The Baroness will have fifty fits,' cried Pea.

'And throw us in the dungeons,' wailed Pod.

'Too many cooks burnt the cake,' Ratty Ragworm gloated gleefully.

'Only magic can save us now,' said Pea. 'Let's get the Spell Book!'

But when they reached the Magic Door it was fast asleep. 'Zzzzz!'
it snored loudly. 'ZzzZzzz!'
'Please wake up,' said Pea but the door snored on. 'Zzzzzzz!'
'Let's throw some water on it,' said Pod. 'When Mrs Slobbersnout does that
to us, we always wake up!'
'Good idea,' said Pea. So they got a large bucket of water from the kitchen
and threw it over the sleeping door.

'**OI!**' roared the door. It was very cross and very wet.
'**WHAT'S THE MAGIC WORD?**' it bellowed.

'Please!' shouted the little pigs.

CREEEAK! Very reluctantly, the door groaned open.

They grabbed the Grand Witch's Spell Book and rushed back
through the dark castle down into the kitchens.

'We need a rising spell,' said Pea as they searched through the book.

The pages seemed to fall open at exactly the right page and they found
the Airy, Scary Spell.

'That's it,' said Pea. 'We need air to make the cake rise.'

This time nothing went wrong and the cake was perfect.
Pea and Pod wanted to write 'Hapy Burfday Baaran' on the top
of the cake in pink icing but they couldn't find a spell for spelling
in the Spell Book.
'The Baron can't read, anyway,' said Pea.

The cake was
ready just in time.
Fleabane, the Baron's
servant, arrived to take it to the
Great Hall for the birthday party.
'This better taste good, little piggies,
or you're for it,' he sneered.
Pea and Pod followed
Fleabane up to the Great Hall.
'Keep your trotters crossed,'
whispered Pea. 'Let's
hope he likes it.'

'H appy Birthday,' everyone sang as the cake was put on the table. '*Yummy,*' drooled a delighted Baron Mugwort. 'I LOVE cake!' and he stuffed it into his mouth as fast as he could.

'This is delicious,' he chomped.

'I want some, Daddy,' said Hortense, holding out her plate.

'No!' roared the Baron, showering everyone with cake crumbs. 'It's my cake. It's my birthday!'

'But you must share, dear,' said the Baroness.

'You greedy pig,' said Horace in utter dismay as the Baron crammed every last crumb into his dribbling jaws.

'Burp!' That was the best cake I've ever eaten!' the Baron snorted.

But then something very strange happened . . .

The Baron began to float gently up out of his throne. 'Eeeeeeek! Stop it!' squealed the Baron as he tried to hang onto the table. But the table tilted and everything crashed to the floor. The Baron lost his grip on the table and in desperation grabbed hold of the Baroness by the ears.

'Let me go, you stupid hog!' screamed Baroness Euphorbia as they both floated up higher and higher.

'Put me down,' she screeched.

'Aaaaah! You weigh a ton, you fat pig!' bawled the Baron. 'I can't hold on any longer!' With an ear-splitting screech, the Baroness slipped from his grasp!

'Eeeeeeeeeek!'

'Eeeeeeek!'

'Eeeeeeek!'

As she fell, the Baroness grabbed the chandelier and swung
violently backwards and forwards.

'I'll maaaaake
yooooooooooooou
paaaaaay foooor
thisssssss!' she shrieked.

She was just getting into the swing of things when she lost her grip . . .
. . . flew out through the window . . .

. . . and landed headfirst in the evil-smelling water of the castle moat.

Ker-Splash!

Meanwhile, the Baron continued to rise up into the rafters of the Great Hall. By now he was covered in cobwebs, soot and bat poo. 'OW!' howled the maddened Baron as his head hit the ceiling. 'Get me down!' ʙ-ᴏ-ɪ-N-G! He bounced off the ceiling and hit a beam. Then he bounced off the beam and hit the wall.

ʙ-ᴏ-ɪ-N-G!　'OW!'　ʙ-ᴏ-ɪ-N-G!　ʙ-ᴏ-ɪ-N-G!

'OW!'

Like a huge yo-yo, the Baron bounced up and down as bats wheeled and squealed around him. Pea and Pod gaped at the scene. The Baroness was screaming in the moat, the Baron was bouncing and bawling in the roof and Horace and Hortense were running around in circles, squealing. The castle was in chaos!

VADOOM!

Suddenly the huge doors of the Great Hall crashed open and in strode the Grand Witch. There was a breathless hush.

With a swirl of magic and a muttered chant, the Grand Witch broke the spell on the bewitched Baron.

'Scary, airy you are no more,
Down you fall onto the floor.'

There was a blinding flash and a thunderous crash. Then in a cloud of dust Baron Walter de Mugwort hit the ground with a mighty thump!

'Happy Birthday, Baron,' smiled the Grand Witch as she helped him back onto his throne.

Pea and Pod looked at each other in horror. They had to disappear fast.

'Hurry, we've got to return the Spell Book,' whispered Pea.

They dashed down to the kitchens, grabbed the very sticky Spell Book and ran back along the dark corridors until they reached the Sorcery Room. 'Please,' they gasped as they stood in front of the magic door. **'NO, PLEASE IS NOT THE MAGIC WORD!'** boomed the door. 'But it is,' squeaked Pea and Pod in dismay. **'NO IT ISN'T, NOT ANY MORE!'** shouted the door. **'BE OFF WITH YOU!'**

Then a dark voice behind them said, 'I think that is **my** Spell Book.'
Slowly the two little pigs turned and found themselves under the terrifying gaze of the Grand Witch.

She had been very surprised to find a talent for magic in the two little pigs. How on earth had they managed it? Airy Scary Spells were extremely difficult and dangerous. These two could be very useful . . .

From her great height she looked down at the trembling piglets and said, 'Henceforth you shall leave the kitchens and assist me in the Sorcery Room. Now follow me, for there is much to be done.'

Pea and Pod scuttled after the Grand Witch in amazement. They could hardly believe their ears – they had become

WiTCH PiGS!

For Lily and James

WITCH PIGS
A JONATHAN CAPE BOOK 0 224 06467 3

Published in Great Britain by Jonathan Cape,
an imprint of Random House Children's Books

This edition published 2005

1 3 5 7 9 10 8 6 4 2

Text copyright © Colin and Jacqui Hawkins, 2005
Illustrations copyright © Colin and Jacqui Hawkins, 2005

RANDOM HOUSE CHILDREN'S BOOKS
61-63 Uxbridge Road, London W5 5SA
A division of The Random House Group Ltd

RANDOM HOUSE AUSTRALIA (PTY) LTD
20 Alfred Street, Milsons Point, Sydney,
New South Wales 2061, Australia

RANDOM HOUSE NEW ZEALAND LTD
18 Poland Road, Glenfield, Auckland 10, New Zealand

RANDOM HOUSE (PTY) LTD
Endulini, 5A Jubilee Road, Parktown 2193, South Africa

THE RANDOM HOUSE GROUP Limited Reg. No. 954009
www.kidsatrandomhouse.co.uk

A CIP catalogue record for this book is available from the British Library.

Printed and bound in Singapore